Kit and Kim

by Susan Hartley • illustrated by Anita DuFalla

Jen has Kit. Kit can kiss Jen.

Jen saw Ben and the pup.
"Look, Ben," said Jen.
"This is Kit. Kit can kiss me."

The pup ran. Kit ran.
Jen and Ben ran.

The fat tan cat saw Kit.
The tan cat ran at Kit.
Kit, the tan cat, the pup,
and Jen and Ben ran.

Kim saw Kit.

"Come here, cat," she said.

"Kim, you have Kit," said Ben.
"I want Kit for Jen."
"Here you are," said Kim.
"Jen can have Kit."

"Come here, Kim," said Jen.
"Kit can kiss you."